ACKNOWLE

I would like to take this time to extend gratitude to everyone that had a hand in me finishing this story. My family and friends that kept me going when I wanted to quit. I also would like to thank my beautiful black people. Without the great accomplishments of those that came before me, I would not have been inspired to write this story in the first place. I want to dedicate this book to the countless black inventors and creators that inspired this story. Whether they are mentioned or not, all of our pioneers played a huge role in the making of this story possible. I also would like to dedicate this story to all of our brothers and sisters who lost their lives in the struggle of oppression. George Stinney, Emmet Till, Sean Bell, Trayvon Martin, Sandra Bland etc. It's sad that there are so many to list. May their souls and the souls of the countless others forever rest in peace. Lastly, I would like to release this book in the memory of my grandmother Shirley Mcdaniels, my twin brother Shaneal Anderson, and my dear friend Alyssa Amadio.

"The Black man is the most feared, most hated, and most imitated."

-Unknown

I

"Get the hell out of here nigger! You know yous don't belong around these parts." Walter Corbett yelled angrily at the black kids riding their bikes down his block. This was a common theme in Castlebrook, especially in 1958. Blacks and whites had a clear understanding to never to cross each other's side of town. The black side of town, known as the "Cogi" section was a very affluent area. Many professionals and business owners resided there. They were economically superior to their white counterparts that occupied the "Seka" section of Castlebrooke. "Seka" was a very impoverished area. This caused a lot of jealousy. Many Seka residents harbored much resentment for the people of Cogi.

"Stay away from those uppity Cogi niggers baby. They're nothing but trouble. Especially those goddamn Bordeauxs!"

Walter explains sternly to his daughter Ethel. "Yes papa." She said in agreeance. "What's so bad about them papa?" She asked. "The Bordeaux's don't know their place. This a white man's world. We brought those people here from their jungle. Now that some nigger-lover politicians throws them a few bones, they think they are equal to us." Walter said as he takes another sip of moonshine from his mason jar. "The world would be a better place if all those animals were erased." He said, ended the conversation.

Meanwhile on the Cogi side of town, Paul Bordeaux stood on his porch with a worried disposition. He is relieved when he finally sees his son George ride up on his bike. "Boy get yo black ass in this house for dinner!" Paul said playfully. "Coming pop." George said apologetically as he bids farewell to his buddies and puts his bike away.

Paul's wife, Delores set the table with baked chicken, mashed potatoes, asparagus, and wine for dinner. "Momma Dear! Time for dinner." She yelled to her mother-in-law,

Helen to let her know dinner was ready.

When Helen came to the dining room, she circled the table while burning sage. This was one of her normal rituals that she would perform to rid the home of bad energy. Magic and voodoo was very dear to Helen. It was one of the only traditions that the Bordeaux family could salvage from their ancestors after slavery.

After Delores said grace, they all started eating. "Pop, we went to Seka today and rode our bikes through that crazy white man,

Walter's grass" George said boastfully.

Paul's take a long drink of wine then slams

his glass on the table angrily. "What the hell I

tell you about going on that side!" Paul said

as he pointed across the table at his son. "Pop

ain't nobody scared of that cracker." George

told his father in a cocky manner. Paul take

off his belt and comes toward George. "So

you think you a man?" He said as he chased

George around the table. Delores and Helen

try their best to break it up. In the middle of

all the confusion, Helen has a vision of fire

and destruction. This causes the arguing to

cease. "What's wrong Mama Dear?" Dolores asked her inquisitively. Helen answered in a very frightened manner. "We are all in great danger. George stay away from those people. You are going to cause more hurt and pain than you'll ever know." George reluctantly promises her that he will obey her wishes. He wasn't the type of kid to back down from anyone or anything. He also had a secret friendship with Walter's daughter, Ethel. A vision from his grandma wasn't going to stand in the way of that.

Weeks later, George disobeyed Helen's warning. After piano practice, instead riding his bike home with his friends George snuck off to Seka to meet up with Ethel. Same spot, 4 pm, Thursday by the creek. "Hey Ethel." George greets her. "How's it going George? Was that you guys that rode through on your bikes a few weeks ago?" She asked rhetorically. "Yeah how'd ya know?" He answered with a smirk. "Well it ain't everyday you see a group of chocolate bars ride through Seka." Ethel said as she stroked her brunette hair behind her ear. They both laughed and walked along the creek.

"Man I really wish things were different." George said frustrated. "Yeah, the color of our skin should separate us." Ethel replied empathetically. "I really don't understand the issue. If we can be friends why can't everyone else? My dad said the world would be better off without you guys but you're the nicest and smartest person I know." George is touched by the compliment. "Aww thanks Ethel." He said jokingly with his hand over his heart. He splashes drops of water from the creek and they began to playfight.

George rode his bike home and Ethel walks back to her house. Once she gets home she is confronted by her father who is visibly angry and drunk. "Were you wrestling around with that voodoo nigger's grandson?" Walter asked demanding answers. "What are you talking about papa?" Ethel asked innocently hiding the truth. "Jasper said he saw you and that Bordeaux nigger from Cogi's son at the creek!" He yelled at her. Ethel knew that if she told the truth about the friendship she would suffer harsh consequences. To save herself, she lied on George even though it killed her to. "He attacked me papa, because his dad hates you!" She said with a misleading cry. This enraged Walter to his breaking point. "That black bastard!" I'll take care of all of them once and for all!" He grabs his shotgun and runs outside to rally up everyone. Ethel ran to her room in utter disgust and guilt for what she had just done.

Walter rounded up all the men in Seka and they all gathered at the town square. Walter began to give a speech to pump everyone up for what was about to happen. "We have been playing nice with these niggers for far too long. This here is a white man's world and it's time we put them in their place! We are going to Cogi and sending a message. Castlebrooke belongs to us. Burn all of their shit down! Anyone who stands in our way, kill them. Bring those Bordeaux's back to me. I have something special planned for those black pieces of shit. Seka is gonna take back what is ours." This got the crowd excited. They all heading to Cogi with their weapons and torches while chanting "White Power!".

Helen had a vision of what was going to take place. She knew it was too late to perform a ritual that could prevent it. She took other measures to rectify the situation. Helen called on the gods using a prophecy ritual. Although Cogi couldn't be protected from what was ahead, this prophecy was to assure that revenge and justice will be carried out.

She attempted to warn everyone about her vision. No one ever took Helen seriously when it came to her visions. "Mama Dear calm down. We'll be just fine, it's all in your head." Paul said assuredly. "Yeah Grammy, and even if anything happens you know I've never been scared of any Seka crackers." George said with a cocky attitude. "That's enough with the sass George!" Delores interjected with a worried expression on her face. She was the one person that would always hear Helen out when she went on her rants. Dolores knew something was different about this one. She felt it in the air that something was wrong. All she could do was grab her Bible and began praying the decats of the rosary.

Later that night, havoc began to ensue on the streets of Cogi. Seka has invaded with full force. Under the leadership of Walter Corbett, the men brought great terror. They burned down and destroyed everything in sight. Anyone that tried to defend themselves were shot and killed on the spot. They destructed the residential areas even worse. People were snatched out of their homes, cars were flipped over, and windows were shot out. It was of apocalyptic proportions.

"Walt! Here goes the nigger's house you were looking for." One of the men alerted him as they approached The Bordeaux house. "Alright niggers, you and your family come on out and get what's coming to ya. You will all pay for what you sons of bitches did to my daughter." Walter yelled at the front door as his men surrounded the house. "What the hell is he talking about George?" Paul asked puzzled. "I'm friends with his daughter, Ethel. I've been sneaking off to see her sometimes. Pop I swear I never hurt her." George answered hesitantly. The whole family responded in perplexity. "I'm sorry y'all. I'll fix this." George said in a discouraged manner. The whole family knew that they had no choice but to turn themselves in. The all held hands and let Helen say a prayer to bless all of their souls.

The mob from Seka captured the Bordeaux family and brought them back to the townsquare. The town was illuminated by the torches held by the Seka residents surrounding the center. All of the members of the Bordeaux family each stood in front of a noose awaiting their execution. "The days of these uppity niggers having the upper hand is over! They've been living in luxury in Cogi while we struggle to make ends meet over here in Seka. This is a white man's world and we're gonna make an example of this nigger, his family, and his voodoo bitch mother!" Walter says to his congregation. Ethel stood off to the side in immense sorry. She never meant for any of this to happen. Ethel was conflicted between the fear of her father and the love she had for George. That is what ultimately compelled her to lie.

George looked out into the crowd and locked eyes with Ethel. She mouthed the words, "I'm sorry, I love you" to him. A tear fell down his face. Although he had so much rage towards her for such betrayal, the love in his heart wouldn't let him hate her. When he looked over at Walter, George's soul boiled with anger. He was enraged by the guilt that his actions were what lead up to this. Unbeknownst to everyone, George hid one of his father's guns in his pants before they were apprehended at the house. George slipped out of his restraints and pointed the gun at Walter. As soon as George raised the revolver, one of Walter's henchmen shot George down with two blasts from a shotgun, instantly killing him. Ethel let out a heart wrenching cry as the crowd unsympathetically cheered.

The remainder of the Bordeaux family sat in shock as they awaited the same fate as George. "You will never get away with this, you spineless bastard!" Helen said to Walter furiously. Walter answered her sarcastically. "Oh, really witch? Well why don't you use your jungle magic to save your family?" The crowd proceeded to join in laughter. "When will you niggers learn your place? I don't know why God even put you in our world."

Walter asked them rhetorically. Helen answered in a devious manner. "Don't worry, the next time someone of your lineage causes black bloodshed, you will get the white man's world that you want so desperately. The only thing that will save the world will be the total demise of your bloodline." Helen said this as she gave Walter a piercing look. Then a bolt of lightning struck the sky. This marked the completion of the prophecy ritual. This frightened Walter. He immediately ordered the commencement of the execution. Each Bordeaux's head was placed in a noose. After a few minutes of struggle, their lifeless bodies hung from the trees. "White Power! White Power!" The crowd chanted in unison as they held their torches high in the air. Once everything calmed down and the crowd left,, Ethel went back to townsquare. She wept over George's body. She expressed her deepest sorrow and she would be forever guilty for what she had done.

II

Castlebrooke was a totally different place in 2018. It was now under the name of "New Seka". Cogi was a thing of the past. A lot had changed since 1958. "New Seka" had progressed economically. They basically stole the entire economic blueprint used by the former Cogi society. The community maintained to have a 100% white population since the destruction of Cogi. Despite the 8 year term of Barack Obama, they kept to themselves politically. They managed to remain a private government that operated on their own accord with all white officials.

Jefferson Corbett, the grandson of Walter Corbett, is the Sheriff of New Seka. His lineage preceded him and he is well respected in town because of the family he comes from. As he's getting ready for work, he yells up to his son. "Cody, before you leave for school remember to take your insulin and give your grandmother her medicine too." Cody finishes administering his own insulin then runs to the top floor to check on an elderly Ethel Corbett. "When's her heart surgery again hun?" Arlene, Jefferson's wife asked him concernedly. "In a few weeks." He sighed and answered. Jefferson was very close to his grandmother. Ethel raised him after both of his parents passed. Ethel suffered from a chronic heart illness and was awaiting open heart surgery. Due to her condition she was often weak and didn't speak much. She mostly would have incoherent conversation as she stared off into space. No one in her family could ascertain what she was trying to say at times.

"Jeffy, I think your nana is getting worse." Arlene expressed to her husband. "What do you mean?" Jefferson asked. "Well the talking to herself is getting crazy. She goes nuts everytime she says some strange word Cogi." She continued. Jefferson brushes her off playfully, "Babe, the woman is on medications. Hallucinations are probably just a side effect. Hell as wild as Cody acts I'm surprised I'm not on any medications myself." Cody hears the exchange as he comes into the kitchen and joins in. "Whatever dad. You're just boring, I have personality." They all chuckle and share a few laughs. Cody grabs his lunch and heads to the door with his dad behind him.

When they open the door, Jefferson is stunned as what he sees. It was like he had seen some sort of phantom being. A moving truck had pulled up to the old McCoy residence. That house had been on the market for months. Nothing could have prepared Jefferson for what he saw once the moving truck parked. A black family was moving across the street. A black person stepping foot in New Seka was unheard of. He turned to Arlene in total dismay, "I don't understand what those people are doing here." He said to Arlene. She did not have an answer. She was just as shocked as he was. "I can't believe it." She said in disbelief. "Do we say anything to them?" She asked Jefferson. He quickly answered, "Hell no! Get back in the house and stay away from those people. I'll let everyone else know to do the same."

Meanwhile across the street, the Younger family were settling into their new home. They were oblivious to the not so warm welcome they were receiving. They moved to New Seka from Philadelphia to be closer to Atlanta for their daughter Kareema's upcoming basic training for the navy. Carl Younger was a Pulitzer Prize award winning author and his wife Geneva was a Psychology professor at UPenn. Besides Kareema, they also had a 13-year-old son named CJ. CJ was a skilled soccer player and considered himself to be quite the thespian with an unhealthy obsession with the works of Shakespeare. They were an esteemed and educated black family. Their demeanor and culture was very reminiscent of the Cogi community.

"Woah! Home sweet home." Carl says in relief as he sets down the last box. Geneva answers reluctantly, "I don't know boo. I'm a philly girl. This down south stuff isn't much of my speed." Carl tries to cheer her up,

"Baby, try to have an open mind. Look at it this way, we're not that far from ATL. Perhaps you'll get a call to join the real housewives of Atlanta." He said jokingly. "Boy don't play with me. I am not that ratchet. I have a Doctorate. Put some respect on my name." She said laughing and slapped him on the arm.

"Dad! Your weirdo son won't help me with this heavy bag." Kareema said to her Carl referring to CJ. "Pops, I just figured GI Jane here would enjoy the exercise." CJ said sarcastically. "You're right. Why don't I test out my Kung Fu grip on your turkey neck." Kareema said jokingly. Carl asks CJ to suck it up and just help her with the bags. "Sure Lady Capulet, it would be my honor to assist you." CJ said in a dramatic Victorian accent. "Who the heck is that little boy?" Kareema asked annoyed but curiously. "Do you know nothing about Shakespeare? She's Juliet's mother in Romeo and Juliet." He informed her. "As if I paid attention in 9th grade English. My dear brother, you need a new hobby." She said playfully concerned. "You won't be saying that when I'm winning a Tony award for my role as Othello on broadway. Are you gonna grab the other side of this bag?" CJ said ending the jokes. "I'm good love, enjoy." Kareema said to her brother as she left him hanging and walked off on her phone.

Once Jefferson got the police station, he was eager to share the startling news that no one was expecting. "Are you guys aware that a black family moved into the McCoy house?" Jefferson revealed to the group.

Officer Arthur responded in disbelief. "How could this happen? Who allowed this?" He asked. "You guess is as good as mine buddy. You know their kind thinks they can do whatever they want once they get a little money and education." Jefferson answered. "Spread the word around town. Limit all interaction with them. Bare minimum conversation. We're gonna contain this the best we can until they get the message and leave." He continued. They all agreed and got prepared for roll call.

Word spread fast about the Younger family's arrival to New Seka. The whole town came to the consensus to ignore and ostracize the "black family". They had every intention of making it hard for them. Carl came up with the idea that everyone in the family should split up and explore the town for themselves and meet people. Geneva went to the local coffee shop called QuickBrew. She approached the counter in a jovial mood. "Hello, may I have a large caramel macchiato with extra cream?" She ordered. The barista gave her no reaction, made her coffee, and pointed to the monitor with her total. Geneva felt uneasy about this but didn't think much of it. She paid for her order and left.

CJ left the house and made his way to the park to play soccer. There were a group of boys playing. Cody Corbett was amongst the group. CJ introduces himself to them. "Hey what's up? Do you guys need a goalie?" He asked politely. "No we're even." Cody answered abruptly. "Well are y'all doing alternates?" CJ asked. "Look, isn't your kind better at basketball anyway? Step off!" One of the kids said sternly. CJ felt disrespected but rather than escalate the situation with one of his witty comebacks, he just walked away.

It was such a nice day, Carl decided to walk to townsquare. He got harsh stares as he walked through town. Carl didn't even notice what was going on. He spotted a flower shop and got the idea to get some roses for Geneva. "Excuse me sir, I'd like 2 dozen of your best Arabian roses. He requested from the shopkeeper. The shopkeeper responded shrewdly, "Boy are you sure you can afford

$75." Carl pulled out a wad of $100 bills. "I sure hope so sir." He answered assuming the man was joking. He gave the man $100 and he examined it thoroughly. Carl was offended by the harsh inquisition. Once the man was done the inspection, he told him to keep the change and took his flowers.

Kareema was quite the introvert. She had no intention of assimilating to life in New Seka. She missed her friends back in Philadelphia. Her main objective was to just countdown the days until she had to leave for training. Rather than explore the boring town, she stayed home. She set up her hookah and listened to Meek Mill. This pastime gave her a feeling of being back home. Kareema had no idea of the discrimination her family was enduring at the hands of the residents.

Across the street at the Corbett house, Arlene was dealing with another episode from Ethel. "Cogi!" Ethel kept screaming in repetition. She tried to calm Ethel down. She had no idea what she was talking about. Her random outbursts seemed to have reached a new height since the arrival of the Younger family. When Jefferson got home, Arlene expressed her frustration. "Hun, your grandma hasn't improved at all." She said. He looked at her with a look of defeat. "Who is George?" She asked him. "I don't know." Jefferson replied. "Well she keeps having conversations with someone named George." Arlene told him as she folded laundry. She was getting frustrated at how nonchalant Jefferson acted in regards to her concerns about Ethel. He never took her condition serious. That was his mechanism to cope with how sick she was. Ethel could've already had her surgery. However, the best cardiovascular clinic was St. Anne's in Atlanta. It was a team comprised of all black doctors. They would never see a black doctor. This delayed Ethel's surgery for months while they waited for an opening with one of the white doctors at the local hospital.

The Youngers were at their home having dinner. Everyone except Kareema were being unusually quiet and acting uneasy about something. She addressed the elephant in the room. "What is the matter with y'all? You usually don't shut up. Now you can hear a pin drop." They all gave each other a weird look. No one had discussed what they experienced that day but they could just sense that something was wrong. CJ broke the silence. "Does anyone notice that something is a tad bit off about this place? Off meaning racist. Because I'm definitely getting Jim Crow, Plessy v Ferguson vibes." He said humorously trying to lighten the mood. Kareema inquired about what happened and each of them told her about the incidents that took place at the coffee shop, florist place, and soccer field.

Kareema was naive to the seriousness of what happened. "Are y'all sure it's that deep? CJ, maybe those kids just did want you to play. Dad everyone checks $100 bills. And mom, if I had a dollar for everytime a barista had bad customer service I'd be rich." She said, trying to rationalize everything that happened. "No something is wrong with this town." Geneva answered seriously. "So, Carl, you didn't noticed that there weren't any black people in this town?" "Well excuse the hell out of me." Carl said argumentatively. They all began shouting at each other. Kareema interrupted the argument. "Chill out! You guys are seriously overreacting. This is still America and we moved down south of all places. Did y'all really expect them to roll out the red carpet for the black family?" Carl calmed down when she began to speak. Kareema was his baby girl and he didn't like to upset her. "Kareema please be careful. We'll wait out the summer and after you leave for the navy we are gonna make our way out of this town." He pleaded with her. "Whatever dad, I'm going to the gym." Kareema said in a dismissive tone.

Kareema took the car keys and walked out the door. CJ followed her out. Although they usually ridiculed each other, he was sincerely concerned about her. "Reem, please watch yourself. These people are crazy." She smile at her little brother and replied, "Don't worry youngboul, I got this. Remember, I'm G.I Jane, I can handle anything." She got in the car and dropped the top as she pulled off.

Her parents watched her from the window as she drove off into the distance.

She headed to the gym in her father's Mercedes. The wind was blowing with the top down as she blasted her favorite song "Focus" by H.E.R. She was so excited while listening to the song that she didn't realize that she was running a red light. Jefferson Corbett was the officer on duty and spotted her. He flashed his lights and pulled her over. "Shit!" Kareema said to herself. Jefferson approached the car. She greeted him as polite as possible. "Good evening officer. I know I totally blew that stop sign like a dummy. I'll take the ticket, it's definitely my bad." Jefferson completely ignored her and responded cold and sternly. "Who'd you steal this car from?. Shocked at what he said, she paused for a second. "Excuse me sir? This is my dad's car" She replied confused. "What sports team does he play for?" He asked in a presumptuous manner.

At this point, She played back everything in her head that her family had warned her about. She was so baffled by the blatant racism that she could barely get her thoughts together. "Give me your driver's license." Jefferson demanded. Kareema hadn't had a chance to get to the DMV to get her Georgia license. She told him that she can show him her military ID. Jefferson wasn't interested in conversing with her any further. "Get out of the car!" He yelled with his hand on his gun. "Officer, I don't understand. I have it right here." She explained to him as she reached for her clutch that she kept her ID in. He raised his gun at her when she grabbed it. As she turned around, Jefferson shot Kareema in her head. She died instantly. Her lifeless body hung over the side of the car. Kareema's blood dropped to the ground and the blood streamed into the soil. He left her body there and went straight home.

The Youngers grew worried. Kareema had been gone for a few hours by this time. Carl got into Geneva's truck and went to look for her. He rode around for about 15 minutes while tracking her phone. He finally spotted his Mercedes on the side of the road. Carl found her slumped over the driver side door.

He was petrified at the sight of his daughter.

"Reema!" He screamed as he ran to the car.

He pulled her out and tried everything he

could to save her but it was much too late.

Carl called Geneva but she could barely

understand what he was saying. When she

finally gathered what he said, she went

hysterical. CJ tried to console his mother the

best way he could. He was equally as hurt by

the loss of his sister.

Jefferson arrived home to explain to his wife what he had done. He lacked remorse for what transpired. He was just more so frightened that he took a life in general. "Arlene!" Get down here." He yelled as he entered the house. She rushed out of bed to see what was so urgent. He informed her that he killed the black girl from across the street. He was shaken up and could barely catch his breath. Arlene reassured him that no one in that town would make a fuss about a dead black girl. Jefferson was afraid that perhaps her father was going to retaliate. He thought of a solution and slowly walked out of the house while Arlene was still talking.

Geneva and CJ were still on the phone with Carl. They were trying to find a way to handle the situation. They knew that there was no one in the town that they could call for help. They also felt that they may be in danger as well. Carl instructed them to pack as much as they could and when he got back they would ride over to Atlanta to seek help.

As they packed, they heard a knock at the door which they figured was Carl. When CJ opened the door, a 9mm handgun was pointed at his forehead. Before he could make sense of what was happening, the gun went off. Geneva ran down the stairs and found CJ grasping on to his last moments of life. As the gunman raised at her, she realized it was Jefferson. She didn't personally know who he was but she recognized it was that white man that was looking at them from across the street as they were moving in. "What the hell is wrong with you people?" She screamed before he pulled the trigger, delivering a fatal shot to her chest.

Carl raced home to gather his family and leave New Seka. Kareema's body was in his backseat. He couldn't bring himself to leave her. He pulled up to the house and ran in hastily to get Geneva and CJ out of there. As soon as he walked in, he received a gunshot to the back of his head. Jefferson was waiting for him, hiding behind the door. Carl struggled for a few seconds before life left his body. Once Carl died, lightning struck the sky. A frightened Jefferson ran across the street. When he got home, a violent earthquake ensued. The Corbetts ducked for cover. After the earthquake stopped, they all fell into a strange sleep. They wouldn't be able to fathom what was about to come.

III

"Hey Ethel, hey Ethel! Wake up!"

George said shaking Ethel. An incoherent

Ethel woke up puzzled. She had been having

nightmares about what happened for years.

However, actually seeing George face to face

was a shock to her. "George?" She asked not

knowing if it was just another dream. "Well it

sure ain't your guardian angel." George's spirit said sarcastically. "What do you want?" She asked. "Oh nothing. Just here to deliver the good news in person. And don't you dare think about apologizing. We're way past that." He said being humorous but stern. "What good news?" Ethel asked. "Those little stunts your grandson pulled fulfilled the prophecy. My people never existed in your pathetic world" He said. Ethel attempts to apologize, "George I never meant-" "Ah ah ah, save the apologies. Not trying to hear any of that. Wow, I see your health isn't that good these days. What a shame. My people could've been a great help with that." He said as he interrupted her apology.

Ethel was stunned at the fact that she was being haunted by George's spirit. He had no compassion. This wasn't the friend she knew. He seemed very harsh and had a vengeful nature about him. George relished in this moment. He was gleeful about her misfortune. "Well don't worry. I'll be right here along for the ride to witness you and your people's demise." George informed her before his spirit temporarily vanished.

"Help! Help!" Ethel yelled out to her family. Her voice was very weak, so she was very hard to hear. The Corbetts all woke up disoriented. Cody woke up and had no clue what was going on. "Did you guys hear something? I think grandma needs help." He said. They all rushed upstairs to her room to see what the matter was. "Granny, what's wrong?" Jefferson asked. Ethel was too shaken up to answer at first. "What is it?" He yelled at her in frustration. "I saw George." She finally answered. He dismissed her. "You were right all along. We should've put her in a home." He turned and said to Arlene.

Arlene addressed the elephant in the room. "Jeffy, what happened last night?" She asked. "I made a mistake, so I rectified the situation before it spread any further." He said mysteriously. "Dad, what did you do?" Cody said, expressing his concern. "I had to get rid of that black family that moved in across the street." Jefferson said putting his head down. "You didn't!" Arlene said in shock. "How will we cover this up?" She asked him. "Only one way." Jefferson said looking at the both of them. He instructed Cody to stay with Ethel while he and Arlene went across the street to cover his tracks.

When they got to the house, Jefferson noticed something that was very peculiar about the scene. The cars were not in the driveway. Nothing looked the same as he left it. When they opened the door, the Younger's bodies were nowhere to be found. Both

Jefferson and Arlene were confused by this. The house was stripped clean as if no one had ever been there. Not understanding what was going on, they just went back home.

"I don't get it. No ambulance or anything came. That I can remember." Jefferson said still puzzled. "Well dad, we all did strangely get knocked out last night. Maybe they came then." Cody said trying to rationalize the situation. "No son, crime scenes don't clear up that fast. Plus, it looks like they were never there. Something strange is going on here." He informed Cody.

As they were talking, they were interrupted by what sounded like a bad car collision. All three of them rushed outside to see what was going on. They saw a minivan with a mother and 2 small children in it, flipped over. They had all died upon impact. The driver of the othe car was seriously hurt but was able to talk. "What happened?" Jefferson asked as he tried to help the man. "I don't know." He said as he drifted out of consciousness. Arlene noticed something odd. She couldn't find any traffic lights at the corner of the streets. She didn't make anything of it. Her main concern was helping the injured man.

While they were helping the accident victims, Ethel went to the window to see what was going on. She couldn't believe the brutal sight of the accident. "It's pretty crazy isn't it? Hope everyone's okay." George said as he appeared behind Ethel. "Hmm, I wonder if a traffic light could have prevented that." He continued being sarcastic. "What do you

mean?" Ethel asked. "Oh, I didn't tell you?

Your daddy's wish came true. Niggers as

y'all like to call us, don't exist. So nothing

made by us exists either. Looks like my

grandma's voodoo really does work. Well

would ya look at that." He replies as he puts

his hands on his hips in with a dramatic

shocked look on his face.

"George we were friends. I'm not like

the others." Ethel said pleading with him.

"Don't give me that! Were you different

when you lied on me, ruined my town, and caused the death of my entire family?" He asked rhetorically. Ethel just looked down in guilt at what he just said. She knew this was true. "Answer me!" He said angrily. "I had to lie. My dad was so upset. There's no telling what he might have done." She explained. "Well in the long run you gave your daddy what he always wanted. There ain't anymore black people. Let me tell you a little secret. Garret Morgan invented the traffic light. He never existed so neither does his invention. I suggest you warn people to be careful on the road. From the looks of it, people probably don't take much of what you have to say seriously these days. But good luck." George told her before disappearing again.

Ethel was shocked by how cold George was being. It was at this point that she realized the severity of what she had done years ago. She allowed her fear of her father to compromise her loyalty to George. This ultimately lead to the destruction of a prominent community and caused the many deaths of innocent people. Her remorse meant nothing to George. The prophecy was fulfilled and he was going to give the Corbetts a front row seat to their own self destruction.

IV

Jefferson returned to the house with Arlene and Cody after assisting with the accident. Everyone involved eventually died. This was very traumatic for the Corbetts. It was unusual for something so catastrophic to occur in New Seka. "Dad, things are definitely not normal." Cody observed.

"What happened to all the street light?" He continued with his concern. Jefferson did not have an answer for him. Arlene was also having a hard time making sense of the situation.

Ethel remained silent through all of their inquisition. She knew that what George said was right. No one would believe her. If she told them the story of Cogi and what happened to the Bordeaux family, they wouldn't listen. Furthermore, if she had admitted that George's spirit was stalking her and that they were on a receiving end of a prophecy that eliminated the contributions of black people, they would've just wrote her off as being crazy and blame it on her medication. "Grandma!" Jefferson yelled when he realized that Ethel was drifting off. He didn't have the patience to deal with one of her episodes at the moment. Cody took her upstairs to avoid the situation escalating any further.

The sun was beginning to go down so Cody flipped the light switch in Ethel's room.

To no avail, the lights did not come on. He looked up and saw that there were no lightbulbs either. Cody screamed for his parents and ran downstairs to tell them what was going on. Jefferson ran to all of the rooms and was met with the same result. He looked out the window and noticed it was considerably dark. The streetlights and lampposts were gone. "Goddamn it! What the hell is this?" He said in frustration.

Upstairs Ethel sat frightened by how everything was falling apart. As she sat in the dark, she reminisced about her child memories with George. Sneaking off to the creek was one of her favorite moments. George saw her pacing into her own thoughts and interrupted her. "Snap out of it Ethel! Those happy days are over. You ruined them, remember?" He said snapping her back into reality. "Why don't you stop this?" She pleaded. "Out of my hands. Can't defy a prophecy. You guys aren't enjoying your white man's world?" He said as he shrugged his shoulders. "People are dying." Ethel said hoping he would having compassion. "Wow, my family and town were murdered. I know exactly how ya feel." George said unsympathetically.

After a few more minutes of conversation, George offered an explanation for the lack of lighting. "Sheesh, it's pretty dark around here. I guess Lewis Latimer could've really came in handy huh?" George said in a matter of fact kind of tone as he scratched his head. Ethel looked at him in confusion. She knew for sure that Thomas Edison had invented the lightbulb. George looked at her in amusement. "Sure, Edison invented the lightbulb, but it would be completely useless without Latimer's discovery of the filament." He informed her. She felt guilty for everything that was transpiring. George assured her that it would only get worse.

Arlene caught the end of Ethel's conversation with George. Of course, she couldn't see him. She assumed that Ethel was just having another episode. Arlene noticed something particularly strange. Ethel usually blurted out random phrases but she never held full conversations like she was just doing. "Mama, who were you talking to up here?" She asked in fearful curiosity. "Nobody." Ethel answered in a soft tone. It was best for her to keep all of this to herself until she figured out how to get her family to believe her.

So that Ethel wouldn't be alone in the dark, Arlene brought her downstairs. Cody and Jefferson were lighting candles around the living room. Ethel sat on the couch. She tried her best to hide her nervousness. Cody was still finding a way to make a logical explanation for everything that was taking place. "Dad, maybe there's something on the news that can tell us what's going on. Let's try the tv and see if the news is on." He suggested. Jefferson tried to cut on the television but it didn't work. He also tried the radio and the same happened. He figured that it was issue with the circuit breaker. Cody accompanied him to the basement to check it out.

George appeared to the right of Ethel on the couch, startling her once again. "They're wasting their time going to the basement. Otis Boykin created the resistor that allows for televisions and radios to operate. Good luck watching Fox News now." He said as he chuckled. Arlene was sitting across from her so Ethel refrained from responding. She wanted to avoid causing any kind of scene. A tear fell down her face. George walked around the room finding things that were invented by black people. Knowing that Arlene couldn't see him, he taunted her.

"Have fun now. If only you knew none of this is gonna work." George yelled at an unsuspecting Arlene. "That's enough!" Ethel said out loud. Arlene was so frustrated at everything that she didn't even acknowledge Ethel's outburst. George was having fun witnessing all of this turmoil. "Wow, this is fun. I gotta stick around to see how this one ends." He said to Ethel as he sat down and kicked his feet up on the ottoman.

Jefferson and Cody came back up from the basement. "No luck with the breaker." He said defeated. "I just bet you didn't have any luck." George said laughing knowing no one could hear him. Arlene figured they should call her sister, Carol to see if they were experiencing the same thing. She tried to dial the number, but her cell phone felt like a rock. It didn't work at all. The same thing occurred when everyone else tried to use their phones. They all stood there puzzled. George sat in the corner taking much pleasure in their misfortune. "Hey Ethel, maybe you should tell them the phones don't work because Henry T. Sampson made the cell phone possible through his discovery of the Gamma-electric cell. Man, I didn't even get to live long enough to see that one. Seems pretty cool though." He said in a very aloof manner. Jefferson decided that they should go out and check on the neighbors. To avoid having to deal with her in public, they left Ethel in the house by herself. George took full advantage of this.

V

Once they left, Ethel found herself in a different environment. She looked down at her hands and saw that they were back to child size. Looking down, she saw that she was wearing the loafers and fringe socks that she use to wear. She also had on a poodle skirt and an Oxford shirt. This was a common ensemble from her childhood. She looked at her reflection in a nearby window of a store and saw that she was a young girl again. Suddenly, someone crept up behind her and said, "Welcome to Cogi". It was George of course. "What is this?" She asked. "I'm gonna finally show you what my people are about." George said as he gestured for her to follow him. "The false hateful things that your dad spread about us were far from the truth." He continued as they walked through the town.

They were interrupted by what sounded like a choir singing. Ethel followed George to St. Rose of Lima church. Once they arrived, they saw the choir singing a common catholic hymn. *Holy, holy, holy is the Lord of hosts. Heaven and earth are full of your glory, Hosana in the highest. Blessed is he who comes in the name of the lord, Hosana in the highest.* Ethel stood in awe as they sang. She had never heard anything so beautiful.

Father Cecil approached the altar to deliver his sermon. "They Lord be with you."

He addressed the congregation. "And also with you." They responded in reverence. "The trials and tribulations we have faced are what have shaped us as a people. God knows the purpose that he put our people to serve. If our ancestors were as inadequate as they portray them to be, we would not have been forced to come here in the first place. We must believe in ourselves. In the words of Marcus Garvey, *If you have no confidence in self, you are twice defeated in the race of life.* As a people of God, we can't let the oppression and ignorance of the white society allow us to feel inferior. Matthew 20:16 states, *So the last will first, and the first will be last.* Look at how well we have established ourselves her in Cogi. Black owned businesses and economic systems have allowed us to thrive tremendously. However, there will be a time when our oppressors will infiltrate what we have. We will have to rebuild our empire over and over again. I tell you people of God here and generations to come, do not grow weary. God created us to be a resilient people. Slavery couldn't break us and neither can Jim Crow. In the years to come, they will continually concoct ways to knock us down as a people. Beautiful black people you must rise from the ashes like a phoenix. Our oppressors fear what they don't understand which causes them to hate us. The perseverance embedded in us by God is what frightens them the most. Their disdain for us has everything to do with them and nothing to do with us. Diminishing our greatness will not alleviate their hateful nature. Until the atone with the lord, those that hurt you will never have a clean heart. If you don't take anything else from what I said today remember this, no matter what adversity comes our way it was already predestined for us to overcome. The lord be with you." The priest finished as the crowd erupted in screams and shouts of "Hallelujah".

Ethel looked over at George with tears in her eyes. She was moved by the priests' sermon. George didn't respond to her and proceeded to escort her out of the church. They took a walk-through center city of Cogi. Ethel saw very professional and high class black people. There were shopkeepers, business owners, doctor's offices etc. even the children playing on the streets were very well dressed. Many people were polite and greeted her. She was totally flabbergasted by this. "Wait, they can see us?" She asked in shock. "Sure, they can. I come from a very welcoming people. You don't have to hide yourself like I do in Seka." George answered. His goal was to prove wrong the misconceptions of Cogi that were perpetuated by the racist people of Seka. They were always portrayed as pompous elitist black people that wanted to see the demise of their white counterparts. In all reality, the main goal of everyone in Cogi was to establish a leveled playing field and be socio-economically equal to other communities.

"I don't think you understand the severity of what you did. The devastation your people caused was catastrophic." George said to Ethel. "I'm sorry for what happened George. You have to believe me. It can't be as bad as you think. We even had a black president." She suggested. Her ignorance angered George. "Sure. Your people throw us a bone and we're supposed to sweep centuries of oppression under the rug." He said sarcastically. "The biggest mistake we made was to trade independence for what we thought was equality. We worked so hard to be accepted by your people that now we don't have anything to call our own. Our conditions in this country have only gotten worse while your people have maintained to have the upper hand." George continued. Ethel was confused. Living in Seka allowed her to be out of touch from the harsh reality of what was going on in the world around her. "I'll show you what I mean." George said swiftly.

The two of them arrived in modern day New York. Ethel felt extremely out of place. She had never been in such an urban area before. "Don't worry. I spared you the embarrassment. No one can see us." George assured her. "Why are we are here?" She asked. "Showing you the error of your people's ways." He replied. They walked by a random playground. There were a group of lightskin girls ridiculing a classmate. "No boy will ever kiss Seraya. She's too fat, black, and ugly." One of the girls said mercilessly. "Tar baby, Tar Baby, Tar Baby." The crowd of girls chanted as Seraya ran away in tears.

"What was that about?" Ethel asked. "Colorism", George informed her. "This is a tactic that your people have used for years to keep us divided." He said. Ethel still did not understand the concept. George had to explain it to her. "For years, black people have divided ourselves by light skin or dark skin. The lighter you are the better you are perceived. The darker you are the harder it is to be accepted." He continued "But being light skin is not a walk in the park either. Many light skin people are ostracized and have to prove how black they are." They both continued to walk. They spotted a group of girls chasing one girl. This time the girls were dark skin and the victim was light skin. "Get back her whitey!" Seraya yelled. They were chasing Keisha, the girl that had previously bullied her. The girls caught up with her and knocked her down. One girl grabbed a handful of mud and rubbed it all over

Keisha's face. "Who's the Tar baby now."
Seraya said vengefully as they walked away.

"Why would anyone want these girls to
fued like this?" Ethel inquired, still not
understanding. "If you keep us divided we
will never be able to unite and fight the real
problem." George answered. "Your ancestors
really know how to divide and conquer a
civilization. Just look at any fallen society of
people in history." He also said. "I'm so
sorry." Ethel attempted to apologize. "What
did I say about apologies? They won't fix

anything. It's too late. George interrupted her as she tried to apologize.

On the next block, they walked into a group of young black men sitting on a porch. Suddenly, they heard police sirens. Ethel asked what was happening and George instructed her to be quiet and just watch. "Get your black asses on the ground." One of the officers demanded. They all complied except for one. "No. We didn't do anything." The young man replied. "Oh really nigger?" The Officer said as he pulled out his baton and hit struck him. Five officers tackled him to the ground and began to use excessive force. One officer put his knee on the young man's head causing his neck to snap.

"You see? Not much has changed in the world." George expressed to Ethel. "Maybe he should've listened to the officer." She suggested to try and justify what happened. George turns to her in frustration and explains. "You still don't get it! It's not about what he did or did not do. It's all about your people feeling the need to be superior. My entire family's lives were taken, and my town was destroyed because your father and people like him feel that my people are somehow inferior to the rest of the world. Whether it was a slave ship, plantation, lynching, colorism, police brutality, or racial profiling, there has always been a system in place to maintain the inferiority of blacks in this country. No matter how much we contribute to this world, you still don't get it. But like I said, save your apologies. We don't exist in your world anymore. Maybe now you'll appreciate us.

VI

At this point, New Seka is in complete disarray. Ethel was abruptly awakened by her family rushing back in the house. They all looked exhausted and appeared to be barefoot. "Dad, what are we gonna do?" Cody asked his father as he looked down and realized that they were not wearing shoes.

"Son I really don't know. I can't make sense of any of this." Jefferson said as he began to cry. Arlene looked out the window and saw nothing but havoc. Cars were flipped over. Houses were on fire. People were screaming in the streets. Riots began to take place. New Seka lost all aspects of civilization.

Ethel remained silent and began hearing voices. "Jan Metzelligar." George's voice whispered to her. She now realized that George was inside her subconscious mind. He explained to her that Jan Metzelligar created the finishing machine for the production of shoes. This was yet another important commodity that they took for granted.

Jefferson noticed that through all the mayhem, none of them had eaten. This was important because of Cody's condition of diabetes. By just looking at him, Arlene could tell that his blood sugar was extremely low. She went into the kitchen and was met with a harsh smell. All the food in the refrigerator was spoiled. It was like the refrigerator had never been cold. It appeared to be a hollow box with a door. Instead of panicking, she attempted to prepare Cody a can of soup. However, the stove did work either. She called Jefferson into the kitchen and had seemed to be at her wit's end. He started slamming cabinets and knocking things off the counters.

Arlene knew they had to eat, especially Cody. She tried to salvage whatever she could to provide a meal for her family. She prepared tuna sandwiches with a few cans of tuna fish she had found in the cupboard.

Mysteriously, none of the potato chips she bought were in the kitchen. She thought nothing of this. Her main concern was making sure that Cody had food. "You need to eat something too." Jefferson said to Arlene. "How can I eat with all that is happening?" She asked as she began to cry. The two began to argue and Cody got in the middle to diffuse the situation.

While they were arguing, Ethel noticed herself zoning out again. George showed up again. He explained to her that T. A

Warrington was responsible for the stove and John Standard invented the refrigerator. As trivial as it sounded, he found great humor in informing her that George L. Crum was the maker of potato chips. "I have to tell them about everything." Ethel said to George. "You do what you want. Nothing will change what you've done. I suppose atonement will benefit your soul." George said nonchalantly.

Ethel resumed back to the argument her family was having. She interjected which startled all of them. She never spoke much, outside of her usual outbursts that they thought were medically induced. "I know why all of this is happening." She said. "What are you talking about grandma? We don't have time for this." Jefferson attempted to dismiss her. "You will listen to me!" Ethel yelled as she slammed her fist on the coffee table. "This is all of our family's fault. This town is not New Seka. It is Castlebrooke. Cogi was a wealthy black community. They actually were more well of than us. My father was terribly racist and jealous of the Bordeaux family. I was friends with George

Bordeaux. I was forced to lie on him and caused the destruction of the town and the death of his family." She continued. Arlene interrupted her assuming this just another meaningless rant. "What does this have to do with anything?" She asked in disbelief. Ethel continued her story. "His grandmother practiced voodoo. She casted a spell on this town. The next black bloodshed by someone in our family would erase black people from existence. I know you won't believe me but George's spirit is here. He told me that the black girl you killed fulfilled the prophecy."

Jefferson saw no validity in this story. "How the hell does that explain us not have shoes, power, or anything else? Where are the damn traffic lights?" He asked Ethel. "Black people not being here also means the elimination of their inventions. Everything your great-grandfather spread about blacks was a lie. Now we are paying for it." She answered.

"You will not disgrace this family name with you mental patient bullshit!" Jefferson screamed at her. He didn't want to accept the fact that his ignorant act had potentially caused the demise of life as he knew it. Arlene and Cody were shaken up by the story. They both were inclined to believe her. Everything she said made sense to them. "Dad, this really does explain a lot. It's not a time to be practical right now. Nothing about this situation is normal." Cody told his father. Jefferson ignored what Cody said and looked out the window gazing at the destruction. He barely recognized New Seka. He played in his head everything Ethel had said about Cogi. He secretly couldn't help but think that perhaps this was karma for what he and those that came before him had done. However, his honor and reverence for his great-grandfather wouldn't let him accept this fact.

Jefferson turned away from the window and detested everything Ethel said. He blamed it on her medication and advised Cody and Arlene to not fall for her antics. They both were confused by his sudden rant. Ethel was frustrated that he still doubted her. Before she could address Jefferson, they all noticed that the house began to shake. It felt like a strong earthquake. They all quickly exited the house. When they got outside, the house started to crumble as if it had no foundation. All of the houses on the block started to do the same thing simultaneously. The entire neighborhood appeared to be in ruins.

VII

The town of New Seka was now in a state of complete squalor. Everything as they knew it was completely destroyed. Buildings had fallen down, and fixtures were knocked over. George neglected to tell Ethel one important detail regarding the prophecy. The elimination of blacks including absolutely anything contributed by blacks. Unbeknownst to most of the New Seka residents, their traditional plantation style homes were all built by black workers. Pretty much the entire infrastructure of the old Castlebrooke was designed by black architects.

The Corbett family stood outside the debris that was once a place that they called home. Many of the neighbors adjacent to them didn't get lucky enough to make it out of their houses in time. Many of them died or were fatally injured. It was very reminiscent to Ethel of the night Cogi was destroyed. The turmoil was all too familiar to her. Ethel's vision was bouncing back and forth from what took place in Cogi to what was currently happening. Jefferson was distraught. The sight of the destruction finally made him realize that everything Ethel said was true. For the moment, his pride made him keep his revelation to himself.

Cody's health was slowly deteriorating. His blood sugar was getting extremely low. It wasn't safe to drive. The roads were full of damaged from collisions and fires were spread everywhere. "How are we going to get help for Cody!" Arlene asked as she wept. "We have to get him to the hospital. Our only option is to take the train from Midtown to Center City." Jefferson advised. He put a sickly Cody over his shoulder while Arlene pushed Ethel in her wheelchair.

The walk to Midtown was excruciating for the Corbetts. Cody's condition seemed to be getting worse. He was very pale and appeared to be experiencing diabetic shock.

Along with this, Ethel was having her own struggle. She hadn't taken her heart medication since all of this started. Not wanting to cause another conflict, she kept her agony to herself. She also was experiencing some mental anguish as well. The route they were taking to the train was where the town of Cogi once stood. Her brain was producing images that they were walking through Cogi instead of the destructed New Seka. "George please stop this." Ethel pleaded. "This is no fault of mine. This is what your people wanted. Simple lesson to be learned about being careful what you wish for." George said with no remorse.

Ethel is brought out of her trans to sound of Arlene screaming Cody's name. Jefferson attempted to stabilize Cody's body from convulsing. After a few minutes of seizing, he finally stopped. However, Cody was in and out of consciousness and was very weak. They had no choice but to keep going to the train station. It was more urgent than ever for them to make it to the hospital. Although Ethel did not draw attention to the fact that she was in pain, Arlene could tell she was in bad shape.

Approaching Midtown, the Corbetts noticed something different about the setting. The train that they were expecting had somehow been flipped over. This was a major setback for them. The train was their only means of transportation to get to the hospital in Center City. "I thought you would get it by now. Did you honestly think we didn't have anything to do with trains? Elijah McCoy invented the lubricating cup for train oil."

George said to Ethel as he appeared to her by standing on top of the wrecked train.

Still barefoot, it was very painstaking to face the reality that they had to walk five miles from midtown to center city. It was very dark outside, and they had no sense of time or direction. "What time is it?" Arlene asked. Jefferson checked his watch and grew even more livid. "Goddamn it! My watch isn't working." Jefferson said enraged. Benjamin Banneker was the creator of the first striking clock. This subsequently led to the invention of the watch. George was very present every step of the way to keep Ethel very aware of how much worse everything was going to get. Walking on gravel and cement was getting very hard for the Corbetts. They finally could see that they were in a safe distance from Georgia General Hospital. They were thankful that this was the one building in New Seka that had not fallen.

Once they made it to the front of the hospital, Jefferson screamed to get some help for Cody. He was fully unconscious at this point. The nurses put him on a stretcher immediately. However, the struggle was far from over. The endocrinologist was on the 8th floor. All of the elevators in the hospital had somehow collapsed. Male nurses and paramedics had to carry Cody and Ethel up eight flights of steps. As they were being brought up, Ethel could see George walking up the stairs behind them. He mouthed the name "Alexander Miles" as he laughed and pointed to the inoperable elevators. She already knew what he was referring to. This was another invention included in the prophecy.

They finally made it upstairs to the specialist. Cody was in a bad predicament. He was in full blown diabetic shock. The doctors tried to give him insulin, but his condition did not improve. "Your son's liver is failing at and abnormal rate and he also needs a blood transfusion." The doctor explained to Jefferson and Arlene. "So, do the damn transfusion! Save my baby." Arlene demanded as she cried in Jefferson's arms.

"I'm afraid it's not that simple. All of the blood donations have somehow disappeared." The doctor replied sorrowfully. The entire Corbett family cried as Cody laid there helpless. As Ethel looked at the monitor screen she noticed something quite peculiar. The screen had the words "Charles Drew: blood transfusion and blood bank". Ethel knew that it was George manipulating the screen to send her a message. The message was taken off when Cody began to flatline. The room went into a panic as doctors and nurses tried to save him. His liver had already failed and most of his internal organs shut down. Arlene and Jefferson were devastated. Ethel felt her body going numb. There was nothing else that the doctors could do to save him. As his lifeless body laid there, they all stood there speechless.

Jefferson then began to have a vision. His great-grandfather, appeared. They were in townsquare of Seka in 1958. Jefferson was getting a front row seat to the carnage that was inflicted upon the Bordeaux family. This epiphany was the final proof that he needed that showed him that everything indoctrinated in him was derived from pure ignorance. "These niggers had it coming son. This is our world." Walter's spirit turned and said to Jefferson. "No!" Jefferson screamed. His resistance resumed him back to reality. He was met with the sight of his son's corpse on a hospital bed. Jefferson then pulled his revolver from his waistband, put it to his head, and pulled the trigger. Arlene and Ethel were hysterical. It was too much for Ethel to take and she collapsed. Doctors began to assess her immediately.

VIII

Ethel was under the impression that she
was dead under she was awaken by the sound
of heart monitors and Arlene praying for her.
She could not move at all. It was as if she was
outside her own body. The room began to
spin and a plethora of visions started racing
through Ethel's mind. She saw slaves being

abducted, Dr. King giving his "I have a dream" speech, to President Obama's being inaugurated. On the outside, Arlene and the doctors saw her going through convulsions and her vitals were fluctuating significantly. "What's happening to her?" Arlene asked. "She is suffering from heart failure and a coronary hemorrhage." The doctor informed her. Arlene started crying and pleaded with the doctor. She had realized that Ethel was the only family she had left. "But doctor, she was due for an open-heart surgery for her condition in a few weeks. Why can't you just do an emergency surgery now?" She asked.

Now in a medically induced coma, Ethel found herself back in Seka. Once again she was a little girl. She was walking through the woods until she met a sight that frightened her. A group of 5 black children were hanging from a tree and being set on fire. Ethel was alarmed when she saw her father, Walter doing this. "Papa, no!" Ethel screamed. "This was the world's design sweetheart. These niggers get out of line, we have to handle them." Walter said as he raised his torch. "You're wrong. This is nothing but hate!" She yelled at her father. He looked at her with an evil scowl. Then he spat in her face. "No daughter of mine will be a nigger lover." He said as he put his hands around her throat.

As her father was choking her, Ethel had another vision. She saw exactly what Jefferson did to the Younger family. These visions also became parallel to what Walter did to the Bordeaux family. She also thought back to what the police did to the young man when she was with George. It was at this moment that she made the correlation between all of the events. They were all connected. She now felt herself losing consciousness from her father's grip and the guilt had her ready to accept death. "Clear!" Ethel heard as a light flashed and she found herself back in the hospital bed. She was brought back to Arlene's conversation with the doctor. He explained that he could not perform the heart surgery. She was baffled by this. The family had filled out paperwork and made payments for the surgery. The doctor

insisted that this was not a procedure that

could be performed.

George appeared at Ethel's bedside. This

time he was accompanied by a man who was

a black doctor. "Who is this?" Ethel asked. "I

am Dr. Daniel Hale Williams, the inventor of

the open-heart surgery." The doctor

responded. A tear fell done her face as she

realized what this meant. She was about to

die and she only had herself to blame for not

having the courage to stand up for what was

right. Succumbing to the doctrine of ignorance spread by her father and his predecessors ultimately caused all of this destruction. All she could think of was the day that she lied and wished that she could've done the right thing.

"Ethel, one thing my people have that yours lack is compassion. Dr. Williams is willing to perform your surgery and try to save you." George said reluctantly. She pondered the option in her head. She then began to think of everything that blacks have been through at the hands of her people.

Kareema's face came to her mind. An

innocent life was taken at the hands of her

family. She decided on the choice that would

offer a minuscule amount of retribution. "No,

let me die." She requested. "I'm trying to

offer you the mercy that your family never

gave mine." George reminded her. "If you

think making yourself some type of martyr

will relieve the harm done, you thought

wrong." George refuted. "Nothing I can do

will reverse what happened. Atleast I can

bring some form of justice on my behalf, this was all of my fault." She confessed to George

Arlene's conversation was cut short by the sound of Ethel flatlining. This was the followed by the hospital building crumbling down. Arlene ran to her son Cody's body and held him tightly. Everyone left in the building died. This virtually turned New Seka into a ghost town. No life was there. It had fallen victim to the very thing it was built on.

Helen Bordeaux kept a specific detail of the prophecy to herself. What she did not reveal was that this entire ordeal was specifically designed for Castlebrooke. She set out to use the town as the catalyst for change from the social injustices that plagued society. Her ultimate goal was to have the "black excellence" of Cogi become prevalent throughout the entire world.

Perhaps the best contribution of the prophecy was the outcome. The main purpose of the destruction of New Seka was to serve as a cleanse to rid the world of ignorance.

Once the prophecy was fulfilled, the rest of

the world changed for the better. There was

no more hatred, discrimination, or racism.

From the most major cities to the smallest

towns, people of all colors lived together in a

way they never did before. Neighborhoods

were now economically prospering. All

people finally worked together. There was no

more violence or division of government.

Society kind of formed itself into some sort

of utopian place rid of all the previous

hardships it once had.

Years had gone by and Castlebrooke was untouched. It was still destructed and full of debris. It was basically left behind by the rest of the world. No contractors saw potential in the site. One day, this all changed. A fleet of pickup trucks with the words *Bordeaux Building Company* pulled up to what use to be Cogi. This company was owned by a group of successful black businessmen and they employed hard workers of all colors. When they got out to observe the site,

Many were apprehensive. "Boss, this place is

trashed. It's literally a ghost town." One of

the men said. He replied, "Well then, let's

give it life."

Made in the USA
San Bernardino, CA
23 March 2019